DISCARD

TWEEN SERIES

# HOW I BECAME
# A FREAK

CHOOSE YOUR OWN

NIGHTMARE

## titles in Large-Print Editions:

# CHOOSE YOUR OWN NIGHTMARE #15

## HOW I BECAME A FREAK

### by Richard Brightfield

**Illustrated by Bill Schmidt**

An Edward Packard Book

Gareth Stevens Publishing
**MILWAUKEE**

**For a free color catalog describing Gareth Stevens' list of high-quality books and multimedia programs, call 1-800-542-2595 (USA) or 1-800-461-9120 (Canada). Gareth Stevens Publishing's Fax: (414) 225-0377. See our catalog, too, on the World Wide Web: http://gsinc.com**

**Library of Congress Cataloging-in-Publication Data**

Brightfield, Rick.
 How I became a freak / by Richard Brightfield ; illustrated by Bill Schmidt.
  p. cm. — (Choose your own nightmare; #15)
 Summary: After being turned into a horrible monster at a carnival house of mirrors, the reader must make plot choices that determine whether or not the freak returns to normal.
 ISBN 0-8368-2072-X (lib. bdg.)
 1. Plot-your-own stories. [1. Horror stories. 2. Carnivals—Fiction.
3. Plot-your-own stories.] I. Schmidt, Bill, ill. II. Title. III. Series.
PZ7.B76523Ho 1998
[Fic]—dc21          97-39606

This edition first published in 1998 by
**Gareth Stevens Publishing**
1555 North RiverCenter Drive, Suite 201
Milwaukee, Wisconsin 53212 USA

Printed in the United States of America

1 2 3 4 5 6 7 8 9 02 01 00 99 98

# HOW I BECAME
# A FREAK

# WARNING!

You have probably read books where scary things happen to people. Well, in *Choose Your Own Nightmare*, you're right in the middle of the action. The scary things are happening to you!

Hanging out at the street carnival sounds like fun. Until you spend a little too much time inside the freaky hall of mirrors . . .

Don't forget—YOU control your fate. Only you can decide what happens. Follow the instructions at the bottom of each page. The thrills and chills that happen to you will depend on your choices.

Are you ready to go to the carnival? Then what are you waiting for? Turn to page 1 and *CHOOSE YOUR OWN NIGHTMARE!*

You've just finished dinner when the telephone rings. You rush to answer it. Your friend Susan is on the line.

"Can you believe it?" she says excitedly. "There's a street carnival over on Elm Street!"

"Great!" you say. "I'll meet you in front of your house. I'm leaving now."

Fifteen minutes later, the two of you are at the carnival. It stretches down Elm Street for two blocks and spills over into a vacant lot at the other end. Music is blaring from loudspeakers, and strings of colored lanterns hang over rows of food stalls and rides. All the carnival workers are dressed as clowns.

You and Susan work your way through the carnival, sampling the Italian sausage and cotton candy as well as trying a few of the scarier rides, like the Centipede and the Doomsday Spinner.

"Look over there. That looks interesting," Susan remarks as you both stagger off the Doomsday Spinner.

*Turn to page 2.*

## 2

Several large carnival trailers are parked in the vacant lot. They are garishly painted and strung with blinking lights. Each has a big sign in front. One reads in large letters: COME IN AND SEE THE DOG WITH TWO HEADS, AND OTHER AMAZING FREAKS OF NATURE.

"Let's go in and see," you urge Susan.

"Yuck! I don't want to waste my money on that," she says, wrinkling her nose.

"How about this next one?" you say. The sign reads: THE AMAZING HALL OF MIRRORS. SEE YOURSELF FAT, SEE YOURSELF THIN, SEE YOURSELF AS A FREAK!

"Give me a break," Susan says. "Anyway, I'm tired. And I think the carnival is getting ready to close. See, they're beginning to turn off the lights." She points to several food-vending carts. The clowns working them are packing up their things and heading out.

"Just a quick look," you say.

"If you want to see yourself as a freak, go ahead," Susan says. "I'll check with you tomorrow. I'm heading home."

*Go to page 4.*

# 4

A carnival clown pops up just as you reach the door to the Hall of Mirrors.

"We're closing up now," the clown tells you.

"Can't I just take a quick look?" you ask.

"Well . . . okay, but make it fast. You've got a minute and a half until closing. If you're not out by then, *you'll be sorry!*"

You don't like the way he says *"you'll be sorry!"* But the clown steps aside, gesturing for you to go in with a broad sweep of his arm.

*Go inside on page 29.*

Manny and Louie drop you into the back of the van. You are still tightly wrapped in your bedcovers.

Sometime later, you arrive at Dr. Quank's laboratory. They carry you inside.

"Put our patient in the usual place," Dr. Quank orders. "And remove the covers."

Manny and Louie put you on a large, circular table in the center of the room and start to unwrap you, pulling the bedcovers away from your face. Suddenly they both leap a foot into the air, their feet heading for the exit even before they hit the floor. They almost knock over Dr. Quank as they run screaming from the building.

"I must make a note to hire new assistants," Dr. Quank says. He walks over to an instrument panel at the side of the room and presses a button. A large glass dome drops down around you from the ceiling. Sparks begin to crackle all over your body. You can feel electricity shooting through you. You beat your hands against the glass, but you can't get out.

*Keep pounding the glass on page 34.*

**6**

"Who's in charge here?" the sergeant demands.

"I am," the clown says, doing a somersault and pulling a flower out of his ear.

"Okay, cut the clowning," the sergeant says sternly. "Take us to the Hall of Mirrors."

The clown leads you and the officers to the back of the carnival where the Hall of Mirrors trailer is parked. He steps aside as you all rush in.

*Flip ahead to page 82.*

You go over to your dresser and pull open the bottom drawer. You find the ski mask you used while sledding last winter and pull it over your head.

You hear your mom and dad talking outside your room. Seconds later, they open your door and peer in.

"See, it's just a ski mask," your dad tells your mom.

"I know what I saw," your mom insists.

"Why *are* you wearing a ski mask?" your dad asks.

"I'm trying to hide my face," you say.

"What is it?" your dad asks. "A skin rash from something you ate? Let me see. It can't be that bad."

"All right, you asked for it," you say, pulling off the mask.

*Turn to page 36.*

**8**

"I guess I'll go with the cowboys," you say.

"Okay, I'll go find Jake. He'll show you the ropes," the clown says.

A few minutes later, the clown comes back with a grizzled character who looks like a *real* cowboy. Your appearance doesn't seem to bother him.

"Here, take this," Jake says, handing you a coil of rope. "You know how to make a lasso?"

"Not exactly," you say.

"Nothin' to it," Jake says, forming a loop in another length of rope and twirling it around his head. "We'll need this to root out some of the renegade strands of barbed wire out on the prairie. Follow me, and we'll track down some of them varmints. Maybe yer looks will put a scare into them."

"They're not alive, are they?" you ask.

"I dunno," he says. "Sometimes I think they are."

The two of you leave the ranch and trek for hours under the blazing sun.

*Trek to page 16.*

"That carnival had no right to do this to you," your dad says. "We're going right down to the police station to file a complaint."

"I can't go looking like this," you say.

"Just keep your ski mask on until we get there. Then we can show them what the carnival did to you," he says.

You go down to the garage with your dad and get into the car. A short time later he parks in front of the police station.

You jump out and hurry through the front door.

"We're here to make a complaint," your dad informs the officer at the front desk.

"Oh, really? And why are you wearing that mask?" the officer asks you.

"That's part of the complaint. You see, this carnival—" your dad starts.

"That's the ski-mask bandit!" an officer just coming into the station calls out, running in your direction.

*Run to page 44.*

# 10

You and your dad are so startled that you stand there unable to move for a few seconds.

"What do you want?" your dad asks the strange men.

"You must come with us," one of them says, pointing at you.

Your dad steps in front of you. "You're not taking anyone anywhere!" he says.

"You don't understand," another man says in a calm voice. "We want to help. There are others in the same condition." He hands your father a card that reads: INSTITUTE FOR THE UNEXPLAINED.

While you're talking, a black van slowly backs up around the corner. The same lettering that is on the card is on the side of the van.

"I still don't think it's a good idea," your dad says.

"Gee, Dad, maybe they're the only ones who can help me change back," you say.

*Trust the men in black? Turn to page 67.*

*If you decide not to, turn to page 84.*

## 12

"Let's go home," you say.

"All right," your dad says, making a sharp turn down Lafayette Street.

"They're still behind us," you say, looking in the rearview mirror.

"When we get home, run into the house and lock yourself in your room. I'll handle them if they try to cause any trouble." Your dad grips the steering wheel tightly.

"Okay, Dad," you say.

When you pull up next to the house, the black van is nowhere to be seen. Relief washes over you.

"I think we lost them," you say as you go into the house.

"I hope so," your dad says.

As soon as you get inside, you hear strange voices in the kitchen.

"I wonder who that can be," your dad says.

When you enter the kitchen, you nearly faint with surprise.

*Turn to page 43.*

You decide to go to the ranch. One of the men in black leads your group through the building to a terrace out back. He points off into the distance toward a group of small buildings at the base of a wooded hill. On the other side of the hill stands what looks like an Indian encampment, with teepees and campfires, their smoke rising in thin columns into the sky.

*Go to page 70.*

**14**

Once you're alone, you slip out of bed and go over to the box. You crawl in through a small opening in the side. A short time later, your parents and Dr. Quank come back. The doctor is delighted to see you in the box.

"This is simply marvelous!" he exclaims.

"How long will it take?" your mother asks.

"Not more than a week or so, I'm sure," Dr. Quank says.

"A week?" your father says.

"A week?" you say from inside the box. Your voice sounds like an echo.

"Well, maybe sooner," Dr. Quank says. "I'll check in a couple of days."

"What do we have to do?" your mother asks.

"Nothing," Dr. Quank says. "Just make sure the patient stays in the box."

You hear your parents and the doctor going off, discussing your case. You'll stay in the box for a while. But not for a whole week.

Suddenly you start to feel a strange sensation.

*To find out what's happening, turn to page 25.*

You run and hide in your closet, shutting the door behind you. You crouch on the floor in the dark, wondering what's going to happen to you now.

A few minutes later, you hear your mom and dad come into your room, looking for you.

"Nobody here," you hear your dad say.

"I'm telling you, it was horrible," your mom says.

"You're sure it wasn't just your imagination?" your dad asks.

"No! It wasn't . . . it was—" your mom starts, and then begins sobbing.

You hope they don't think to look in the closet. Luckily you hear the door shut as they leave the room.

You open the closet door a crack to make sure they've really left. Then you go over and look in the mirror again. You gasp and turn away.

You look just the way you did in the last mirror at the carnival! You've got to get back there! You grab a T-shirt from the top of your dresser and run to the window.

*Rush to page 37.*

# 16

"There it is—over there!" Jake suddenly exclaims. "Barbed wire! When I give the signal, toss yer lasso over it and pull."

Jake crouches down low as he advances on the wire. You do the same and follow behind him. "Now!" he shouts, standing up and tossing his lasso. Both your lassos loop around sections of the wire.

"Pull! Pull for all yer worth!" Jake cries.

You pull as hard as you can.

"Harder!" Jake says. "Harder!"

The wire starts to give. You begin stripping away a length of it. Suddenly several long strands rise up and twist around in the air. They do seem as if they're alive.

"Uh-oh!" Jake says. "We're in for it now."

*To find out what he means, turn to page 65.*

The ozone box, Dr. Quank explains to your father, is a large cardboard box lined with aluminum foil.

"The box concentrates the cosmic rays inside, completely neutralizing the bad bagel rays emanating from the patient," Dr. Quank says.

"Bagel rays?" your father says.

"My own terminology," Dr. Quank says. "Now, if the patient will just climb into the box, we can start the treatment."

"I'm not going to do it," you mumble from deep under the covers.

"I think our patient may be a bit shy," Dr. Quank says gently. "It's my experience that if we leave the room, the patient might give it a try."

"All right, we're leaving the room now," your dad says for your benefit. "No one will see you if you get up and climb into the box."

*If you climb into the box, turn to page 14.*

*If you stay in bed, turn to page 57.*

## 18

"I think I'll go with the Indians," you say.

"All right, then, your guide will be Running Eagle," the clown says.

An American Indian, dressed in a loincloth, deerskin leggings, and moccasins, comes out of the ranch. He wears a large feathered head-dress. He begins dancing in a circle.

"You can join in the dance if you want to," the clown says.

*Do you want to? Turn to page 68.*

You approach the figure and see that it's a boy about your age.

"Can I help?" you ask, bending over.

The sobbing stops. After a short pause, the boy mumbles from under the bucket, "No one can help me. I'm a monster for life."

"You're not the only one. Take off the bucket, and I'll show you," you say, unwrapping your T-shirt.

The boy tips the bucket to one side and peers out. You can't see all of his face, but you can tell right away that it's similar to yours.

"Yipes! Another one!" the boy exclaims when he sees you. He jumps up and darts down the street into an alley, holding his bucket at an angle—just enough to see where he's going.

*If you go after him, turn to page 24.*

*If you stay on the vacant lot, turn to page 48.*

"Ugh!" the officer cries out, dropping his gun and shielding his eyes with his hands.

"That's disgusting!" shrieks the officer behind the front desk, diving for cover. The other officer makes a dash out the front door of the station.

"I'm putting the mask back on," you call. "You can come out now."

"You're sure?" the officer under the desk says, looking out cautiously. "I'm afraid we're going to have to put you in solitary."

"For what?" you ask.

"If you were loose in public, it could cause widespread panic," the officer says. "I'm keeping you in isolation until I can find out what's going on."

"I'll tell you what's going on," your dad says. "It's all the fault of that street carnival."

"You're telling me a carnival is responsible for this?" the officer says.

"A mirror at the carnival," you put in.

"We'll find out about *that*," the officers say, leading you away to a cell.

*Go to your cell on page 58.*

"What is that?" you ask.

"That's the quick fix chamber," the man replies.

"It looks like a rocket," you say worriedly. "Are you sure it's safe?"

"We've had no complaints," the man says. "Now, if you'll just climb inside, we can get this whole thing over with."

You squeeze through the circular door and look around. In the center of the room inside is a thickly padded reclining chair. You try it out.

"That's right. Just sit back and relax," the man calls through the circular door just before slamming it shut.

In front of you is some kind of instrument panel with lights blinking on and off.

"Have a good ride," a voice says from a speaker somewhere over your head.

*A good ride?* You try to jump up from the chair, but suddenly you hear a roar. You feel as if a million giants are sitting on top of you.

*Turn to page 54.*

"You were great, stupendous, sensational!" the clown says. "I can offer you a permanent position with the carnival including all benefits. We have one of the best health care plans in the business. And don't forget the retirement plan."

"I don't know if—" you start.

"This is your golden opportunity to be in show business," the clown goes on. "You'll love it. Just ask FidoFido here."

FidoFido, the two-headed dog, is jumping up and down with excitement.

You wonder. What else are you going to do with your life, now that you're a freak?

*If you decide to stay with the carnival, turn to page 83.*

*If you decide not to, turn to page 69.*

## 24

"Stop!" you call out. On your bike, you start after the boy. It doesn't take long for you to catch up with him. He stops, out of breath.

"We should stick together," you say. "When did this happen to you?"

"A few days ago, at that miserable carnival," he says. "It was over on Dacey Street. I heard it had moved here. I guess I missed it."

"Were you in the Hall of Mirrors?" you ask.

"Yep. I see the same thing happened to you," the boy says. "I guess we're done for."

As the boy is talking, something off to the side of the alley catches your eye. It's a pile of junk put out for a trash pickup. In the center lies a mirror. It's the same size as the ones at the carnival.

"Let's try something," you say, dragging the boy over to the mirror. You position him in front of it. "When I count to three, take off your bucket," you say.

"I'll try anything," he says.

*To find out what happens, turn to page 35.*

Dr. Quank was right! You can feel the cosmic rays concentrating around your body. Soon you feel as if you're floating in the air. Only the top of the box keeps you from rising to the ceiling.

Wow! This is fun. You had the doctor all wrong.

Sometime later, you look out through the opening in the side of the box. Your room is foggy. You can hardly see the door to the hallway. That's strange. You stick out your head. You glance down and realize that the floor of your room is missing. It's like looking into an abyss.

You pull your head back in and crouch in the corner of the box. What is this? Some kind of nightmare or something?

You bet it is!

**The End**

## 26

The dog with two heads has a friendly bark—or barks—and its tail is wagging. It runs up to you and then runs a little way down the street. It does this several times. You realize that it wants you to follow it. You decide to see where it wants you to go.

After several blocks you hear a familiar sound. You turn a corner—and there it is, up ahead: the street carnival! You can see the crowds of people milling about.

You stop. You certainly don't want to go any farther. If the people see you, they might panic. The dog barks at you a couple of times, then moves off to the left and down a deserted alley.

*Now where is it going?* you wonder.

*Follow the dog to page 49.*

You run down to the door at the end of the corridor and peek out. The outer office looks deserted. The guard is nowhere in sight. Your guess is that he's probably several blocks away by now, overcome with panic.

A door on the far side of the office is also ajar. You run over and find that it leads outside. It's now late at night.

You slip through the door and dash across the street. As you do, you realize that you've left your ski mask back in your cell. Too late to go back for it now!

Suddenly you hear a screech.

*To find out why, turn to page 30.*

## 28

"Take me back to the carnival!" you cry. "If I can look in that mirror again, this . . . condition might go away!"

"All right," your dad says. "Run down and jump in the car—and put your ski mask back on."

A short time later, you arrive at Elm Street. But there is no sign of the carnival.

"You're *sure* this is the right place?" your dad asks.

"I am," you say. "The Hall of Mirrors was in a trailer in that vacant lot over there."

*Hurry to page 59.*

You hurry through the doorway. You're the only one inside the exhibit. Full-length mirrors with wide, gilded frames line each side. The first mirror makes you look like a beanpole twisted into a tall S shape. In the next one, you balloon out like a giant beach ball, with a head the size of an orange. Another mirror makes you look all twisted around—definitely like some kind of freak.

"We're closing. Time to go," the clown calls out, standing by the door.

"Okay, I'll be right there," you say, still fascinated by how weird you look in the mirrors.

"You must go!" The clown is shouting now.

"Just one more look," you beg.

"No time—we're closing in three seconds!"

You're on your way out, but as you reach the door, you lean back and take a quick look in the mirror by the exit. The mirror's frame is creepy, carved in the image of a monster. Your face is horribly distorted. The clown wrings his hands and dashes out.

You wonder why the clown didn't want you to look in the mirrors after closing.

*To find out what happens next, turn to page 53.*

## 30

Several cars slam on their brakes as you cross the street. Others crash into them from behind. Some drivers jump out and run away screaming.

"Hey, I'm sorry!" you call as you reach the other side. "I can't help the way I look."

You run down the sidewalk toward Susan's house. When you get there, you climb over the fence into her backyard, then up to the tree house you helped her build.

You hide there for the rest of the night and most of the next day. You find a bottle of stale soda on the edge of the tree house platform. You're really thirsty. You drink the whole bottle—stale or not. As you do, a feeling of relief washes over you. You can't really explain it, but suddenly you feel a lot better.

That afternoon, you hear the school bus stop at the corner. You know Susan will be coming home from school. You wonder if she'll come out to the tree house.

*To find out if she does, turn to page 55.*

# 32

You run back and jump into bed, pulling the covers over your head. A few seconds later, your mom comes back with your dad.

"Come out from under there and let's have a look," your dad says.

"I'm not coming out!" you say.

"We don't want to force you," your dad says. "Come out when you're ready."

Your mom and dad take turns sitting by your bed. During your mom's turn your dad comes back with some news. "Dr. Quank is on his way over," he says.

"I don't want a doctor. I'm not sick," you say.

"I think he should look at you anyway," your mom says.

Sometime later, Dr. Quank arrives.

"Come out for a few seconds so the doctor can get a look at you," your dad says.

"No!" you say, burying yourself deeper.

"Just a peek," the doctor says, lifting up the edge of the covers.

*Turn to page 75.*

You go through the front door of the building and find yourself in a large entry hall. A number of people are already there. Most have paper bags over their heads, but a few wear ski masks like yours. A podium is set up at the side. One of the men in black steps up to it and says, "Attention, everybody. No one is to remove their head coverings—for the time being at least. You will have your choice between what I call the 'quick fix' and going to the ranch. Both have their dangers."

"What dangers?" someone calls out.

"I'd rather not say at this point," the man in black says, "except to tell you that your conditions could get better . . . or much worse."

A groan goes through the crowd.

"All of you who want to try the quick fix should stand by that door at the far end of the hall," the man goes on. "The rest of you will be taken to the ranch."

---

*If you try the quick fix, turn to page 79.*

*If you go to the ranch, turn to page 13.*

# 34

Dr. Quank presses another button, and you start wildly changing into all sorts of shapes. First you look like a giant spider. Then an oversized gopher. It makes you feel really weird, but at least it's not painful.

Every once in a while you change back into your regular, precarnival self—but only for a few seconds.

Finally, when you're completely exhausted, Dr. Quank turns off the current.

"We're getting there. A few more treatments and you'll be your old self," he says. "But not too much treatment all at one time. Right now you need some rest."

He presses a button, and the glass dome lifts off you. You feel dazed as he leads you to a side room. It looks like a standard hospital room with a bed, a side table, and a TV fastened to the wall. You lie down on the bed and try watching TV for a while, but you're too tired. You quickly doze off.

*Maybe you'll wake up on page 64.*

"One, two, three," you count.

You pull off your T-shirt as the boy lifts the bucket off his head. You both catch a glimpse of yourselves in the mirror. At the same moment, you smash the mirror with a rock you've picked up off the ground.

The mirror shatters into a million pieces.

Nothing happens.

"Darn!" you say. "I thought it might work."

"Yipes!" the boy calls out. "On top of everything else, I'm bleeding." A piece of glass from the mirror has cut his face.

"Sorry about that," you say. Then you realize you're bleeding, too. A piece of glass has cut your hand.

You both sit down on boxes and start to cry. After a while, you reach up to wipe your eyes—and find they're back in their right place! You look at the boy. His eyes have also moved.

*To find out what's happening, turn to page 46.*

# 36

Your dad's mouth drops open and his eyes bulge as he staggers a few steps backward. Your mom covers her face with her hands. "My baby," she sobs.

"H-How did this happen to you?" your dad stammers.

"I don't know!" you cry. "I woke up this way. I was all right when I went to bed last night—I think."

"You're sure?" your mom says, still shielding her face.

"Well, sort of sure," you say. "I didn't look in the mirror before I went to bed, but—"

Suddenly you realize what has happened. It was the mirror at the carnival. The way you look now was the last reflection of your face in the Hall of Mirrors—seconds after the carnival closed.

"It was that mirror at the carnival—*it* did this to me!" you say. "I've got to get over there and make it change me back!"

"I think we should go right to the police," your dad says. "This is a criminal act."

---

*If you go to the police, turn to page 9.*

*If you look for the carnival, turn to page 28.*

You open your window and climb out, using a vine outside to get down to the ground. You run to the back of the house and jump onto your bike. You pedal off in the direction of the carnival as fast as you can, your T-shirt wrapped around your head and blowing in the breeze.

As you turn the corner at Mulberry Street, your friend Jimmy comes running out to meet you, waving his arms for you to stop.

"Oh no! Not now!" you say to yourself.

"You're certainly going somewhere in a hurry. What's up?" Jimmy asks.

"I can't tell you right now, and—"

"And why do you have that T-shirt wrapped around your head like that?" he interrupts.

"It's keeping my face warm," you say.

"On a hot day like this? Give me a break," Jimmy says. "Come on, what gives?"

Before you can stop him, Jimmy grabs the end of your T-shirt and pulls it halfway off.

*To find out Jimmy's reaction, turn to page 62.*

## 38

When you wake up, it's dark. A large campfire is burning a short distance away. Tom-toms are beating out a steady rhythm.

You can't explain why, but this time you feel you have to dance. Running Eagle comes over to you with a large, helmetlike mask in the shape of a buffalo head. "Here, put this on," he says.

At first you don't want to put on the mask. It looks heavy and uncomfortable. But then you realize that it will cover your own horrible-looking face.

The mask slips on easily. Strangely, it feels very light, and you can see through the eyes. You start dancing around the fire with the Indians. You dance and dance—for hours. You can't stop. You have to keep moving, like the buffalo. *Moving, moving!*

Finally everything goes black.

*Wake up again on page 73.*

You wrap a sheet around you and slip quietly across the lab. You peek through one of the other doors. Inside, a strange creature is sleeping on its back, its feet in the air. It has the body of a large cat but the head of a man. You wonder how it got into *that* condition.

You go over to the door that leads outside and open it. You have no idea where you are. Boarded-up buildings line the far side of the street. At least it's deserted.

Fortunately, since you are only wearing a sheet, the weather is warm. If someone *does* see you, they'll probably think you're a ghost.

You start down the broken pavement. You have no idea where you're going, only that you're getting away from crazy Dr. Quank.

Then you hear a couple of dogs barking from the shadows. Or maybe it's one dog and an echo. They seem to be barking in unison.

A few seconds later, the dog trots out under a streetlamp. It's then that you realize it's one dog with two heads.

*To find out about the dog with two heads, turn to page 26.*

Suddenly you find yourself in a cage fronted by wire mesh. On the other side of the mesh is a crowd of people. A clown is standing to one side. "And here we have, ladies and gentlemen, one of the world's most gruesome freaks," he announces.

*"Aghhh!"* Some of the people scream. Others faint. Several look sick.

"Gross!" yells a woman with two young children.

"Horrible!" shriek a young couple, running out of the trailer with their hands over their mouths.

After a few minutes you stagger back through the opening behind you. The clown is there, waiting.

*To find out what the clown says, turn to page 23.*

# 42

You wait until the carnival closes for the night. The clown puts a cloth over your head so that you can't see and leads you back to the Hall of Mirrors.

He faces you toward the mirror that turned you into a freak. Then he starts counting down. "Five, four, three, two, one, bingo!"

He yanks the cloth off your head. You look into the mirror. Your reflection is normal!

"Great!" you say, reaching to touch your image. Your hand goes right through the glass. "Look," you say. "My hand goes right through the—"

Suddenly something grabs your wrist on the other side of the glass—and yanks you through!

---

*To find out what this is all about, turn to page 66.*

Three of the men in black are having coffee with your mom.

"What are you doing here?" your dad says.

"We've been discussing the situation," one of them says.

"The discussion is over," your dad says.

"I'm afraid it's not going to be that easy," the man says, turning to you. "You've stumbled on a cosmic conspiracy. Aliens disguised as clowns have invaded our planet. We've got to stop them before they turn everyone into . . . well, duplicates of you."

Both your mom and your dad gasp.

"I didn't mean to—" you start.

"We know that," the man says. "But right now it's important that we keep you in isolation—and perform certain tests. It's for the good of your country—and planet, for that matter."

"All right, I'll go," you say bravely.

*Turn to page 72.*

# 44

The officer grabs you. "This is the perp who robbed the First National Bank yesterday!" he says. "And you thought you got away with it!"

Another officer moves in from the other side. "Stand there and don't make a move," he says, taking out his revolver. "Now take off that mask."

"You won't like it," you warn.

"Take it off, or I'll take it off for you!" the officer barks.

"All right, you asked for it," you say, pulling off your mask.

*Brace yourself and turn to page 21.*

"Yes—what is it?" the sergeant asks.

"We've spotted the carnival over on the other side of town—in the old factory district," the officer says.

"I wonder what it's doing over there," the sergeant says. "That's a bad neighborhood."

"Probably trying to lie low," the officer says.

"All right, we already have a search warrant," the sergeant says. "I want to get a look at the mirror that's caused all this trouble."

The officers take you out to a waiting police car in front of the station. As soon as you get in, it speeds off. Fifteen minutes later, you arrive at the carnival.

As soon as they see the police car, most of the carnival clowns run away as fast as they can. In fact, there's only one left. The officers jump out of the car and grab him.

*Turn to page 6.*

# 46

"I think we're back to normal!" you say, standing up.

"I think you're right!" the boy says. He feels around on his face.

"Maybe old-fashioned bloodletting is curing us," you say. "My hygiene teacher, Mrs. Murray, said that bloodletting was how they used to treat medical conditions, in the old days."

"And we did it by accident," the boy says, grinning from ear to ear with a now-normal mouth.

You both give sighs of relief and start laughing hysterically. The two of you are sure to be good friends from now on.

**The End**

"Mom! What's the matter?"

You get out of bed and go over to the mirror by your desk. What you see makes you jump. "Agh!" you cry out, looking behind you to see what horrible monster is looming over your shoulder. But there's nothing there! You look back at the mirror. The monster is you!

All your features are twisted out of shape. One eye is on your forehead, and the other is where your mouth should be. Your mouth, now a vertical slash, has moved to the side of your head. Your lips are bumpy and green. Your nose has replaced your left ear, and your ears are where your nose should be.

You have a powerful urge to run back to bed and dive under the covers. Or maybe you can find something to hide your face.

*If you head back under the covers, turn to page 32.*

*If you look for something to hide your face, turn to page 7.*

*If you run into the closet and close the door, turn to page 15.*

# 48

You decide to stay at the vacant lot. Maybe you can find some clue about where the carnival went after it left here.

You search around, but you can't find anything. Then you hear a dog barking from the edge of the lot. You look over and see that it's a two-headed dog. A two-headed dog! The carnival had a two-headed dog.

The dog starts to run away, then comes back and barks at you. It does this a couple of times—it clearly wants you to follow it.

The next time it runs away, you go after it. The two-headed dog leads you on a merry chase across town.

*To find out where it leads you, go on to the next page.*

You follow the dog. It leads you to the back of a carnival trailer. There's no one there. The dog runs over and scrapes its paws on the door.

The door opens. A carnival clown appears, silhouetted in the doorway. His nose is a large red ball, almost half the size of his head, and his shoes must be at least size fifty. His face breaks into a broad smile.

*Go to page 81.*

The mirror shatters into a million shards. Suddenly you snap back to your normal self. You put your hands over your eyes and stumble outside. You don't want to take the chance of looking in another distorting mirror.

"Wow! I'm all right!" You jump up and down for joy. "Officers, I'm myself again. You can come out," you call in through the door.

All you can hear inside is hysterical laughter.

A short time later, the officers do come out. You look at them in horror. They've all been turned into freaks.

You run away down the street, happy that you're okay.

But unfortunately you're in for seven years of bad luck for breaking the mirror.

**The End**

# 52

You decide to stay in the lab. You go back to bed and fall asleep again.

Dr. Quank wakes you up in the morning, all excited. "I have it. It came to me in my sleep," he says. "I've figured out the proper instrument settings. Quick, get back on the table in the laboratory."

You do as he says. The glass dome comes down on you again. Dr. Quank bends over his control panel, making some fine adjustments. "There it is!" he says, pushing the buttons.

The electricity goes through you again, but this time you quickly turn back into your pre-carnival self.

"You've done it, Doctor," you say as the glass dome lifts off you. You thank him and go home.

The cure is *almost* perfect. But there will be one time in Mrs. Turner's civics class when you turn back into—*you know what!*

**The End**

You run out of the trailer. All the carnival lights have been turned off. The clown who let you in has vanished. You walk along Elm Street. All the rides have vanished, too. That's *really* strange, you think. How did they move them out so fast?

You go home through the dark, deserted streets, not seeing anybody on your way. You slip quietly into the house and go up to your room. You don't want your parents to know you're coming in so late.

*Turn to page 76.*

# 54

Your distorted shape becomes even more distorted. In fact, you're pressed flat as a pancake. The process seems to go on forever.

Finally the roar stops, and the giants release you. You float up from the chair. In the evenly distributed light, the ceiling of polished metal acts like a large mirror. You look at yourself as you float around the chamber. You seem completely normal! The quick fix worked!

*Turn to page 80.*

A few minutes later, you hear the screen door at the back of Susan's house slam shut. You wrap your head in a small blanket you found in the tree house.

Moments later Susan's face appears at the edge of the tree house platform. "Don't get scared," you say. "It's me, here, under the blanket."

Susan recognizes your voice. "Why are you doing that with the blanket?" she asks. "And why weren't you in school today?"

"You remember that Hall of Mirrors I went into at the carnival?" you say.

"Of course I do. What has that got to do with anything?" she asks.

"I still look the way I did in one of the distorting mirrors," you say.

"I don't believe it—let me see."

"I'm telling you, you don't want to."

"Let me see, or I'll pull that blanket off you."

"All right, here goes," you say, sticking your head out.

*Turn to page 63.*

# 56

Finally the van comes to a stop, and the back door opens. The men in black usher everyone out.

The van is parked at the bottom of a high hill. At the top stands a large building somewhat like a castle. But it has too many windows to be a real castle. Some distance to the right of it is a large, square tower with no windows at all.

You all start up a long pathway, moving single file toward the building.

*Turn to page 33.*

You remain where you are. When your parents and Dr. Quank come back into the room, Dr. Quank looks in the box. "No one in there," he says.

You burrow deeper under the covers.

"What do we do now?" your mom says.

"If the patient won't cooperate, there's nothing I can do," Dr. Quank says. "Unless we remove the patient to my laboratory."

"I don't know," your mom says. "Maybe we should wait awhile."

"No, it must be done immediately, or things could take a nasty turn for the worse."

"A turn for the worse? That's not good," your mom says nervously.

"I'll have my assistants transport the patient. It won't hurt a bit," the doctor assures her.

You listen hard. You can hear Manny and Louie packing up and removing the ozone box. Then they come back for you. Louie grabs one end of you—still wrapped in the bedcovers—while Manny grabs the other. They carry you down to the van waiting out front.

*Turn to page 5.*

# 58

You sit in your cell on a blanket-covered cot. A dim light comes from a tiny window high up in the wall. You take off the ski mask—at least no one can see you in here.

Sometime later, you hear a noise outside your cell. The door opens slightly. You see a guard holding a tray with a cheeseburger and soda. At least they're going to feed you. You hope you can eat in the condition you're in. You have to feel around your head to find out where your mouth is.

The guard reaches in to hand you the tray. As he does, the bright light from the corridor strikes your face. Your guess is that they haven't told the guard what you look like. He screams and drops the tray, running back down the corridor as fast as he can.

You look out of your cell. In his terror, the guard left the door at the end of the corridor open. This could be your chance to escape—if you want to.

---

*If you decide to escape, turn to page 27.*

*If you decide to stay in your cell and see what happens, turn to page 78.*

Your dad drives over and parks at the edge of the lot.

"Let's take a look," he says. "Maybe we can find a clue as to where it went."

"Suppose someone sees me," you say nervously.

"There's no one around," your dad says.

You get out of the car and walk over to where the trailer was parked. "See, here are the tire tracks it left," you say.

Suddenly three men dressed in black appear around the corner of a nearby building. They walk toward you.

*Turn to page 10.*

Unexpectedly, you find that you can breathe underwater with your new, freaky head. You manage to get your dad out of the car and up to a platform under the pier, saving him from drowning.

"Those men must think we're done for," you say. "As far as I can see from here, they've left."

Later, you become a champion scuba diver. Not needing a tank gives you a great advantage, though you still wear your face mask so that others can't see what you look like. Occasionally you remove it underwater. That's very good for scaring off sharks.

**The End**

# 62

A shocked look comes over Jimmy's face before his eyes glaze over and he sinks to the ground in a dead faint. Luckily he lands on the grassy strip at the side of the street.

Maybe I can get changed back before he comes to, you think, wrapping the T-shirt tighter around your face. You start off again in the direction of the carnival.

Minutes later, you arrive at the now-vacant lot where the carnival was held the night before. The lot is deserted, but you can hear muffled sobs coming from somewhere. You look around and spot a figure crouched at the base of a nearby tree. It has a bucket over its head—and the sobbing sound is coming from under the bucket!

*To find out who it is, turn to page 19.*

Susan gives you a blank stare. "Well?" she says.

"Don't you see?" you say.

"See what?"

"What a freak I've turned into!"

"You look about the same to me," she says.

"I do?" You feel your head. "You're right!" you exclaim. "I've turned back into myself! I wonder if it was that soda . . ."

"Did you drink that whole bottle of stale soda? Yuck. I can't believe you."

"You're not listening. I'm myself again. I've got to go home and show my mom and dad!"

"If you say so," Susan says.

Everything is all right again. But only as long as you don't drink any more soda!

**The End**

# 64

You wake up sometime during the night. The TV is still on, tuned to a really boring program. It gives you enough light to see around the room.

You lie there for a while, now wide awake, wondering what to do. Dr. Quank's treatments *may* be working, but you're not sure.

Growing restless, you slip out of bed and approach the door of your room. It's unlocked. You open it a crack and look out. The laboratory is dark except for shafts of dim light coming from several partly open doors around the room. You guess that there are other patients receiving treatments.

On the far side of the room is a door that may lead to the outside.

*If you decide to sneak out of the laboratory, turn to page 39.*

*If you decide to stay for more of Dr. Quank's treatments, turn to page 52.*

"What's the matter?" you say.

"There's wire all around us! Run for yer life!"

You follow Jake as best you can, stumbling across the rocky ground. A large tangle of barbed wire lies right in front of you. You try to turn in the other direction. But as you do, you trip and fall into another patch of wire behind you.

The barbed wire wraps around you. The more you struggle, the more it tightens its grip. The barbs bite into your flesh.

"Owww!" you cry out. "If I escape, I'll never complain about anything again—even about being a freak!"

But it's no use. No one ever escapes the Wired West.

**The End**

# 66

Now you're on the other side of the mirror. You try to get back through, but you can't! Your nose bumps the hard glass. You're imprisoned!

At least your reflection is still normal. You turn and look around. Everything else is distorted, as though you were looking at things in a fun-house mirror. You see people walking around. They all look the way you did a few minutes ago.

Oh, great. You're trapped in another dimension where you look normal to yourself but like a freak to everyone else.

*That's* how much worse things can get!

**The End**

"I might as well go with them," you say. "They may be able to help me."

"Be careful—and keep in touch," your dad says as you climb into the van.

The door of the van closes behind you and the van starts to move. You look around. Several people are seated on a bench inside. They all have paper bags over their heads with eye slits cut out. You sit down in a vacant spot and try to make conversation. But no one will say anything. The ride is bumpy and seems to go on forever.

*Go to page 56.*

# 68

"Uh—I think I'll just watch," you say.

"If you want it that way," the clown says, signaling to Running Eagle to stop.

The Indian gestures to you. "Come," he says, starting toward the teepee village in the distance. He jogs along in his moccasins, putting his weight on his toes. You have a hard time keeping up.

You're worn out by the time you get to the village. You lie down in front of a teepee and doze off.

*Wake up on page 38.*

"Thanks for the offer, but I don't think it's for me," you tell the clown.

"What a shame," the clown says with a sigh. "You'd be such a great attraction. I guess now you'd like to look at yourself in the mirror again. You see, I know all about you—how you took one more look in the mirror than you should have. Big mistake!"

"Can I give the mirror a try, really?" you beg. Maybe another look will turn you back into your old self.

"You'll have to wait until the carnival closes for the night," the clown tells you. "If you want to change your condition, you'll have to pick exactly the right moment to look—or things could get worse."

"Worse?" you shriek.

---

*How much worse can they get? Turn to page 42.*

# 70

Several clowns appear from around the side of the building, leading a group of horses. Clowns? You wonder if they have any connection with the clowns at the carnival.

"You will go to the ranch on horseback," the man in black says to your group. "I'm assuming that all of you know how to ride."

You've never actually ridden a horse, but you've always wanted to. This should be fun.

The clowns help you climb up into the saddle of one of the horses. Suddenly the horse bucks violently. You could swear that you saw flames coming out of its mouth. Then the horse goes galloping off, with you clinging to the saddle.

*Gallop to page 77.*

# 72

After a year in a federal laboratory, they are still running tests on you. They keep reassuring you that they'll find an answer soon.

**The End**

It's early morning when you wake up. The Indian village is some distance away. When you struggle to your feet, you find yourself standing on all fours. You're surrounded by real buffaloes.

The buffalo mask you put on for the dance has somehow fused to your head. It *is* your head.

The grass tastes delicious, even better than the sausage you had at the street carnival. But then, you've forgotten about the carnival. You don't even know that you've turned into a buffalo. The only thing you can remember is roaming the wide plains with the herd.

**The End**

# 74

"We'll lose them on the waterfront," your dad says confidently. "I know it like the back of my hand."

When you get there, your dad zooms the car in and around the side streets.

"The van is still following us, Dad," you say. "But it's getting farther behind."

"Good," your dad says. "I think we'll lose them on this next street."

Your dad makes a sharp right turn and heads forward at top speed.

"Watch out!" you say. "This is a pier!"

"A pier?"

Too late. Your car goes sailing off the end, crashes into the water, and sinks to the bottom of the river.

*To find out what happens, turn to page 61.*

"Oh my!" The doctor gasps. "This *is* something unusual. Do you have a picture of how the patient normally looks?"

"There's a snapshot on the desk. It was taken at school," your dad says proudly.

Dr. Quank looks at your picture. He pulls thoughtfully on his beard. "I think I see the problem. And I have a solution. I'll have my assistants bring up the box."

"The box?" your dad asks.

"Yes. I call it the ozone box."

"I thought the ozone was something in the air that protects us from the sun," your mom says.

"Yes, well . . . it does that, too," Dr. Quank says. "But I thought it a rather good name for the box."

A short time later, the doctor's assistants, Manny and Louie, bring up the box from a van parked in front of your house.

*Turn to page 17.*

# 76

You climb into bed and pull the covers over your head just as your mother opens the door and turns out the light. Your head feels strange on the pillow—you can't seem to get into a comfortable position. But you're really tired, and soon you fall asleep.

The next morning, your mom comes in to wake you for school. You poke your head out from under the covers.

Your mom takes one look at you and runs out of the room screaming!

*To find out why, turn to page 47.*

The next few minutes are a blur. The horse dashes toward the ranch in the distance. You hold on for dear life.

Finally the horse slows down and trots peacefully the rest of the way to the ranch. A group of clowns is waiting there. They're clowns, all right—but all wearing boots and Western-style ten-gallon hats. On one side of the ranch house is a sign that reads: INDIANS THIS WAY. On the other side of the house, there's a sign that reads: COWBOYS THIS WAY.

One of the clowns walks over to you. "Do you want to go with the cowboys or the Indians?" he asks.

*Cowboys, turn to page 8.*

*Indians, turn to page 18.*

# 78

You lie back down on the cot and try to make yourself comfortable. After a while you fall asleep.

The next morning one of the officers opens the door to your cell. Fortunately you've already put your ski mask back on.

"We caught the real ski-mask bandit last night," he says. "So I guess you're in the clear. But we still have a few questions to ask you."

The officer takes you to the interrogation room. Two other officers are waiting there.

"We've had other complaints about this carnival," one officer says. "None of them is quite as serious as yours, but there are enough to put together a pattern. The carnival keeps moving around the city, never staying in one place for more than a day. Now, tell us exactly what happened."

You go through the whole story—from the time you went to the carnival until you woke up the next morning.

Just then another officer rushes into the room. "Hey, Sarge! I have some vital information about this case," he says.

*Turn to page 45.*

"I think I'll try the quick fix," you say.

The man in black looks startled. You wonder if you've made the right choice.

"Yes, yes, the quick fix," he hisses, an evil gleam in his eyes.

Before you can change your mind, one of the other men comes over and hurries you to a side door. He leads you down a long corridor in the direction of the large, windowless tower you saw from the outside. Every hundred feet, you pass through heavy doors that close and seal off the hallway behind you. You are definitely getting worried.

You emerge into what looks like an airplane hangar. In the center is a large cylinder stretching up to the ceiling. A small circular door opens at the base.

*To find out what the cylinder is, turn to page 22.*

## 80

"You are now in Earth orbit. Have fun," the voice says from the loudspeaker.

"When do we return to Earth?" you ask.

"Return to Earth?" the voice says. "No one has programmed me to do that."

"No! No!" you scream. "I want to go home!"

You may or may not get home, but one thing is sure. You'll be in orbit for a long, long time.

**The End**

"Ah, splendid," he says. "You've come to audition for the freak show. Come right in."

You walk up the few steps to the door of the trailer and go in.

"Right this way," the clown says, leading you to a narrow opening in an inside partition. He gestures for you to squeeze through.

You might as well. You can't see what you have to lose.

---

*To squeeze through the opening, turn to page 41.*

# 82

"It was the last mirror on the end that did this to me," you say.

"This one here?" the sergeant asks, gesturing at the mirror.

"That's right," you say.

"Hey, Sarge," one of the officers calls over, "get a load of me in this mirror. I look like a kangaroo."

Another officer is laughing hysterically at his own reflection. Even the sergeant starts looking at himself.

"Hey! Cut it out!" you holler. "You're supposed to be helping me."

In desperation, you kick the mirror that turned you into a freak.

*To find out what happens next, turn to page 51.*

You decide to stay with the carnival. Soon you're famous. The carnival is receiving performance requests from all over the world.

Your life is certainly looking up. Now you're afraid you might turn back into your old run-of-the-mill self.

Everything goes well until one night, on a flight to Bulgaria, your plane disappears from radar as it intersects with an unidentified flying object. It seems your fame has spread to other planets as well.

Don't worry, though. The aliens will safely return you to Earth after a command performance on the planet Zor.

**The End**

## 84

"I don't trust these guys at all," you say.

"I don't either," your dad says under his breath. "Let's get out of here."

Two of the men move off to the sides. They're trying to surround you. You and your dad back up toward the car.

"Jump in, quick!" your dad says.

As soon as you're inside, your dad puts his foot on the accelerator. The car zooms off, nearly running over one of the men in black.

You're a block away when you realize that the black van is following close behind you. Your dad makes several sharp turns at high speed but can't shake them.

"What'll we do now?" you say.

"We could head home, or I could try to lose them down on the waterfront," your dad says. "What do you think?"

---

*If you head for home, turn to page 12.*

*If you head for the waterfront, turn to page 74.*